CW00841067

Poor Mister Booh

Mister Booh likes to eat things which make him fat. One day he makes a silly mistake and he starts to eat even more.

Enid Blyton's

Poor Mister Booh

illustrated by Edgar Hodges

Published in Great Britain by World International Publishing Limited,
An Egmont Company,
Egmont House, P.O.Box 111 Great Ducie Street, Manchester M60 3BL.
Printed in DDR. ISBN 0 7235 4450 6

A CIP catalogue record for this book is available from the British Library.

Mister Booh was a fat little man who lived in Chubby Cottages, down Lemon Lane. He was fat because he ate lots of butter, eggs, cream and milk, and he liked being fat. He said it made him feel good-tempered.

One day he went to a meeting to decide whether or not Lemon Lane should be widened. There was a very narrow place in the middle of it and carts couldn't pass each other there, but were always getting stuck. So Mister Booh and all the other folk living in Lemon Lane went to talk about it and to see what should be done.

Mister Booh put on his new rubber boots, because it was raining. He took his brown gloves, too, because his hands got cold very easily. Then he went off to the meeting.

Everybody talked a great deal and they all enjoyed themselves very much and felt very grand. Nothing was decided, but they said they would meet again the very next week and have another talk.

Then they all went out into the hall to put on their outdoor things to go home.

Mister Booh put on his rubber boots, and took his brown gloves from the hall-stand. Then he said goodbye to everyone and started off for home.

He put on his gloves, and they somehow seemed rather big. His boots flip-flapped as he went too, and this surprised Mister Booh very much. He looked down at them and saw that they really hardly fitted his feet.

"Well, that's funny," he said. "Have my feet gone smaller? These boots fitted me well enough when I bought them last week." Then he looked at his gloves and was more surprised than ever. They seemed too big as well!

"Oh dear, I'm getting thin!" said Mr Booh. "I wonder why that is? I must be ill. Yes, that's it, I'm going to be ill, and that's why my hands and feet are thinner and my shoes and gloves too big."

He was very worried, and decided to call at the doctor's and tell him.

So when he came to Doctor Come-in's house, Mister Booh went and knocked on the door.

Doctor Come-in was at home. "What's the matter with you?" he asked Mister Booh. "You look worried."

"Yes, Doctor, and I *feel* worried," said poor Mister Booh. "I've got much thinner in a week."

"Dear me, you look as fat as ever to me," said Doctor Come-in.

"Well, I'm not," said Mister Booh, and he showed the doctor how very much too big his boots and his gloves were.

"That will show you how much thinner I've got in a week, because when I bought these new last week they fitted me very well indeed."

"Dear, dear, you must be wasting away," said Doctor Come-in.

"Well, never mind; we'll soon put you right. You must eat plenty of cream, butter and eggs, and drink lots of milk. Then you'll soon be as fat as ever again."

"Well, Doctor Come-in, I eat all those now," said Mister Booh.

"Eat twice as much then," said the doctor, "and come and see me in a week's time."

Mister Booh went home, still very worried. He ordered twice as many eggs and twice as much butter, cream, and milk as usual. His milkman was so pleased. Mister Booh stayed indoors all that week, because he wanted to give himself the chance to get fat again.

And do you know, when the day came for him to go to the next meeting about the widening of the narrow place in Lemon Lane, he could only just get his rubber boots on! And he split the gloves – so that shows you how much bigger his hands had grown.

Mister Booh was delighted. He walked to the meeting, took off his rubber boots and gloves, and went into the dining-room, where everybody was talking nineteen to the dozen.

After the meeting was over, and still nothing was decided at all, they went out into the hall again to get their things. Mister Booh found his boots, but dear, dear me, what a surprise he got to find he couldn't *possibly* get them on! They were about two sizes too small. And as for his gloves, well, he couldn't even get his thumb into the thumb-hole!

"But I can't have grown so much fatter just in the meeting," he cried, quite frightened. Everybody crowded round him to see what was the matter, and he told them.

"Oh, please," said a small voice, "I think I can explain."

Mister Booh turned round and saw a very tall, thin man with large feet and hands. He was wearing rubber boots and gloves that had split down the side.

"Well, explain then," said Mister Booh.

"You see, last week someone went off with my new rubber boots," said the tall man in a meek voice, "and my gloves too. He left me his small boots and gloves instead, and I had a dreadful time getting home in the boots. I didn't know whose they were, but I thought perhaps they would be brought back to this meeting and they were. I've got them on now.

"Those that you have now are *really* yours, Mister Booh, and I can't think why you can't get them on."

"But I know why," groaned poor Mister Booh. "Oh dear, oh dear. I didn't guess I had on gloves and boots belonging to a bigger person than me."

"I thought they were my own, and I was very much worried because I felt sure my feet and hands had gone thin. So I went to the doctor and he told me how to get fatter and now that I have my own boots and gloves back again I'm too fat to get them on."

"Poor Mister Booh," said everyone. "Whatever will you do?"

Well, of course he couldn't do anything except walk home in his stockinged feet and carry his gloves instead of wearing them. And he was very much afraid that he wouldn't be able to wear his other shoes either, or any of his gloves, and even his new suit would be too tight for him.

Mister Booh went past the doctor's house very quickly because he knew that Doctor Come-in would be expecting him that day. He didn't want to go in and explain that he really hadn't been getting thinner after all, and was now much too fat. No, the doctor would laugh if he knew that.

So he went sadly home, making no noise at all in his stockinged feet, wishing and wishing that he hadn't eaten such a lot of butter, cream, eggs and milk, and thinking of all the new clothes he would have to buy.

Poor Mister Booh!